P9-CSW-758

Shark Tooth
Tale

Shark Tooth Tale

by ABBY KLEIN

illustrated by
JOHN MCKINLEY

THE BLUE SKY PRESS
An Imprint of Scholastic Inc. • New York

To Bonnie,
the best mentor and friend anyone could ever ask for.

To Baxter:
You will always be in my heart.

Love, A.K.

THE BLUE SKY PRESS

Text copyright © 2006 by Abby Klein
Illustrations copyright © 2006 by John McKinley
All rights reserved.

Special thanks to Robert Martin Staenberg.

If you purchased this book without a cover, you should be aware
that this book is stolen property. It was reported as "unsold and
destroyed" to the publisher, and neither the author nor the
publisher has received payment for this "stripped book."

No part of this publication may be reproduced, stored in
a retrieval system, or transmitted in any form or by any means,
electronic, mechanical, photocopying, recording, or otherwise,
without written permission of the publisher. For information
regarding permission, please write to: Permissions Department,
Scholastic Inc., 557 Broadway, New York, New York 10012.
SCHOLASTIC, THE BLUE SKY PRESS, and associated logos are
trademarks and/or registered trademarks of Scholastic Inc.
Library of Congress catalog card number: 2006004382
ISBN 0-439-78458-1
10 9 8 7 6 5 4 3 2   06 07 08 09 10
Printed in the United States of America   40
First printing, September 2006

CHAPTERS

I have a problem.

A really, really, big problem.

I saw this awesome fossilized

Megalodon tooth at a store

at the mall. I really, really want it,

but my mom and dad won't buy it

for me, and I don't have enough

money to buy it myself.

Let me tell you about it.

CHAPTER 1

Pretty Please with a Cherry on Top

"Hey, can I go look around Treasures of Time?" I asked my mom during our latest trip to the mall.

"Not that dumb store again," my sister, Suzie, whined. "I am sooo sick of that place. You make us go in there every time we come to the mall, and it is so boring."

"It is not dumb," I said. "It has really cool fossils, and rocks, and treasures. You just don't like it because it doesn't have lip gloss or anything pink."

"What did you just say, Wimp?" Suzie asked, sticking her nose in my face.

"Get away from me, Weirdo. Your breath stinks," I said, holding my nose.

"Well, your whole body smells," Suzie said, poking me in the chest with her finger.

"All right. Enough, you two," my mom said, stepping in between us. "You're making a big scene."

"So, Mom, can we go to the store?" I asked. "I want to see if they have anything new."

"I don't think so, Freddy. It's getting late. I still have to go home and make dinner."

"Pretty please with a cherry on top? Just for five minutes. I swear. You can even time me, and I promise I'll leave when five minutes are up."

"Yeah, right," Suzie muttered under her breath. "As if."

"Oh, all right," my mom said. "But just for five minutes, Freddy, and then we really have to go home."

"You're the best," I said, hugging her.

I ran over to Treasures of Time and stopped in my tracks as soon as I saw it in the window. I had never seen anything like it before. "No way," I whispered as my mouth dropped open in amazement.

"Why aren't you going in?" my mom asked when she and Suzie caught up to me.

I just stood there staring.

"Uh, hello," Suzie said, waving her hand in front of my face. "Earth to Freddy. Earth to Freddy."

"Huh? What?" I mumbled.

"What are you doing, honey?" my mom

asked. "Don't you want to go in? Remember, I said you only have five minutes."

"Look at that," I said, pointing. My eyes were growing bigger by the second.

"Look at what?" Suzie and my mom said together.

"That shark's tooth," I answered, pointing into the store window.

"A shark's tooth," Suzie said, laughing. "I can't believe you are drooling over a stupid shark's tooth. You already have a bunch of them at home."

"But I don't have *that* one."

"What's so special about that one?" my mom asked.

"It's a fossilized Megalodon tooth. They are very rare," I continued. "I've always wanted one."

"Well, your five minutes are almost up,"

Suzie butted in. "Are you going to go inside or not?"

"Yeah. I want to ask the guy how much it costs. It's awesome!"

I went inside and ran to the cash register. "Umm . . . Excuse me," I said to the guy behind the counter. "How much is that Megalodon tooth in the window?"

"We just got that in today. It's cool, isn't it? It's more than a million years old. I almost didn't even put it out. I thought I might just keep it for myself," he said, laughing.

"How much is it?" I asked again.

"Fifty dollars," the guy said, smiling.

"Fifty dollars? Did you say fif . . . fif . . . fifty dollars?" I stuttered.

"Yep. Worth every penny."

My heart sank. Fifty dollars! I didn't have fifty dollars, and my birthday and Christmas were months away. I couldn't wait that long. Somebody would buy it before then. What was I going to do?

"OK, Freddy," my mom called. "It's time to go. Come on."

My mom came over to the counter. "Freddy, you promised, remember? It's time to go. Your five minutes are up."

"But I have to get this today, Mom. If I don't, someone else will come along and buy it. Will you get it for me, pleeeaaase?"

"Not today, but if you really want it, you have money in your piggy bank. You can buy it for yourself."

"But it costs fifty dollars."

"Fifty dollars!" Suzie said. "Fifty dollars for a silly tooth. That's crazy!"

"That does seem a bit much for a shark's tooth," my mom agreed.

"Not really," said the guy behind the counter. "You don't see these too often. This is the first time we've ever had one here in the store. They are rare."

"You see, Mom," I said. "It's really special. I have to have it."

"Like I said," my mom continued, "if you want it, then you have to pay for it with your own money."

"But I don't have fifty dollars."

"Well then, I guess you can't get it," Suzie

interrupted. "Can we go now, Mom? It's been a lot longer than five minutes."

"Yes. Come on, Freddy. Time to go."

I couldn't leave the store without it. "But Mom, wait," I called after her. "How about an early birthday present? I promise I won't ask you for anything else for my birthday."

"Absolutely not, Freddy. End of discussion. You already broke one promise you made to me today. You told me you would only be in this store for five minutes, and we've already been in here for ten. I'm not staying one more minute. Daddy will be home soon."

As we started to walk out of the store, the guy behind the counter called after me. "Hey, kid, I know how much you want that tooth. I can hold it for you for one week."

"Really?" I said, turning back, my face brightening.

"Yep. One week."

"Gee, thanks!" I said. "I'll be back."

As we left the store, I took one last look at the tooth shining in the window. I decided I had to get that tooth, some way, somehow, if it was the last thing I did. But I only had one week to do it.

CHAPTER 2

I'll Ask Dad

That night at dinner, I decided to tell my dad about the shark's tooth. I was sure he would understand why it cost so much, and why I needed to get it right away.

"Hey, Dad, guess what?"

"What?"

"You know what I saw at the mall today?"

"What?"

"Guess."

"Oh, I don't know."

"Just guess."

"Freddy," my dad said, "I'm not a mind reader, and I'm not in the mood to play twenty questions. Just tell me already."

This was not going as well as I had planned. He seemed to be getting irritated, and the last thing I needed was for him to be grumpy. That would not help my case at all. "OK, I'll tell you. Drumroll, please," I said as I tapped my fingers on the table.

"Oh please," Suzie moaned. "I can't take it anymore. He saw a shark's tooth!" she blurted out. "A stupid, dumb shark's tooth."

"Hey, that's not fair. I was going to tell him! Why'd you have to tell, you Bigmouth?"

"What's the big deal?" Suzie answered. "Like I said, it's just a dumb old shark's tooth."

"It's not just any shark's tooth, Dad. It's a fossilized Megalodon tooth."

"Oh, really?" my dad said. "You don't see those very often."

Now I had him. "I know," I continued. "It's soooo cool. I wish you could have seen it."

"I'd like to see it sometime."

It was now or never. "How about tomorrow after you get home from work? You could take me to Treasures of Time, and I could show it to you, and then we could buy it."

"Hold on there just a minute, Mouse. Who said anything about buying it? I just said I wanted to see it."

Rats. I almost had him.

"Excuse me, Freddy," my mom said, joining the conversation. "But we already talked about this at the mall."

Great. I could see my plan slowly slipping away. I had to think fast.

"Yeah, Mom said it was really expensive,

and if you wanted to get it, you had to buy it with your own money," Suzie piped up.

There went the plan. Right down the drain.

"Freddy?" my dad asked. "Is that true? Is that what your mother told you?"

"Yep," I mumbled.

"What was that? I didn't hear you," my dad said.

"That's exactly what Mom told him," Suzie said. "I was there."

"Suzie, I don't need your help here. I'm talking to Freddy, not you."

"Yes, that's what Mom said," I grumbled.

"Well then, why are you asking me to buy it for you? Do you think that if you don't like the answer Mom gives you then you can just come to me for a different answer?"

"I was hoping," I muttered under my breath. "Really hoping."

"Do we not live in the same house?" my dad continued. "Do you think we don't talk to each other? Your mother and I support each other one hundred percent. If your mother said no, then the answer is no."

"But . . ."

"No 'buts,' Freddy. End of discussion," my dad said.

"That's exactly what she said at the mall."

"You see? We can even read each other's minds," my dad said, smiling at my mom.

"Great. Just great," I said, slamming my fork on the table. "Now I'm never ever going to get it."

"Freddy, please do not slam your silverware on the table," my mom said. "You might scratch the table, or the fork might fly out of your hand and hurt your sister."

That sounded like a good idea to me. A

good punishment for always sticking her nose in places where it doesn't belong.

"Why are you getting so upset, Freddy?" my dad asked.

"Because you won't buy it for me, and I don't have enough money to buy it myself."

"How much does it cost?"

"Fifty dollars!"

"Woooeee," my dad said, whistling. "That *is* a lot of money."

"Especially for some silly shark's tooth," Suzie chimed in.

"It's not silly!" I yelled in her face.

"Ewww, gross, you little pig. You just spit some potato in my face," she said, wiping the corner of her eye.

"Yeah, right. Whatever."

"Hey, Mom, Dad! Make him say he's sorry," Suzie whined.

"OK, enough," said my mom. "I'm tired of listening to the two of you fight. You've been at each other's throats all afternoon."

"Freddy," said my dad, "how much do you have in your piggy bank?"

"I just counted my money when I came home from the mall this afternoon, and I only have thirty-two dollars."

"Only? That's a lot of money."

"But it's not enough to get the Megalodon tooth, and by the time I save up enough money, it will be gone! The guy's only holding it for a week."

"Hold on a minute. Let's figure this out," my mom said. "If you have thirty-two dollars saved up, and you need fifty to buy the tooth, then how much do you still need?"

"I didn't know I was in school," I moaned. "I'm not in the mood to do math problems."

"Come on, Freddy," my dad said. "Your mother's just trying to help."

"Well, unless you are planning on giving me the rest of the money, figuring out how much I *don't* have is not much help. It just puts me in a worse mood."

"OK. I'll help you out," said my dad.

"Really?" I asked excitedly. "You'll give me the rest of the money?"

"No, I didn't say that," my dad answered. "But maybe your mother and I can help you think of ways to earn the eighteen dollars you still need."

"Earn it? What do you mean, earn it?" I asked. "I don't have a job."

"That's a great idea!" my mom agreed. "You could do some big chores around the house, and we'll pay you for your work."

"What kind of big chores? And how much would you pay me?"

"Oh, I don't know," said my dad. "Maybe you could sweep out the garage or wash the car, and we could pay you two dollars per chore. How does that sound?"

"Two dollars! It will take me forever to earn the money, and the tooth will be gone. That doesn't sound like a very good idea to me, and those chores are really boring."

"Nobody said earning money was easy," my dad said.

"Well, why don't you just think about it," said my mom.

"Yeah, that's what I'm going to have to do," I mumbled. "Come up with my own plan." I hit my forehead with the palm of my hand and muttered, "Think, think, think."

CHAPTER 3

What's the Plan, Stan?

The next day, I couldn't wait to get on the bus and tell my best friend, Robbie, about the Megalodon tooth. He would think it was supercool, and I knew he would be able to come up with a good plan for getting the rest of the money. Robbie is a genius.

I ran up the steps of the bus. "Hey, Robbie, guess what?" I said as I plopped down on the seat next to him.

"What?" he asked.

"You're never going to believe what I saw at Treasures of Time yesterday!"

"What? Tell me already," Robbie said, shaking me.

"A fossilized Megalodon tooth!"

"A Megalodon tooth? No way," Robbie gasped, his mouth hanging open.

"Yes way."

"A *real* Megalodon tooth?" Robbie asked, looking me right in the eye. "Are you sure it wasn't a replica?"

"Oh, I'm sure," I answered, grinning from ear to ear.

"That is sooo cool," Robbie said and sighed.

"Hey, what's sooo cool, geek?" Max butted in, mimicking Robbie. "Did you get new shark underwear?"

"For your information," said Robbie,

"we're talking about a genuine fossilized Megalodon tooth."

"A what?" said Max. "You are such a nerd!"

"A real Megalodon tooth," I answered. "A Megalodon was an ancient shark that lived more than a million years ago."

"That does sound cool, Freddy," Jessie said, as she leaned over the back of my seat and joined the conversation.

"Did you know that the scientific name for the Megalodon means 'great tooth'?" Robbie said in his know-it-all voice. I actually don't mind when Robbie talks like that because he really does know it all. He is like a walking encyclopedia of science.

"No. Only science geeks like you know that," said Max.

"What did a Megalodon shark look like?" asked Jessie.

"It looked like a great white shark only a lot bigger," I said, stretching my arms out.

"Yeah," Robbie agreed. "About four times bigger! It was actually one of the largest predators that ever lived on Earth, including the dinosaurs."

"Really?" said Jessie.

"I read in a book," Robbie continued, "that they could be anywhere between forty to eighty feet long. That's bigger than this bus!"

"Well, the tooth was pretty big," I said. "I mean, I'm sure it could fit in my pocket, but it was almost as big as my hand."

"They needed big teeth," Robbie continued. "They ate whales and just gulped them down in large chunks."

"Can you all just stop talking about this?" Chloe squealed and covered her ears. "I'm never going to swim in the ocean again!"

"Oh, you don't have to worry," said Robbie. "The Megalodon is extinct. Because sharks don't have bones in their bodies, the only thing left of these monsters is their giant, fossilized teeth."

"I've just got to have that tooth!" I moaned, leaning back against the seat.

"So? What's the problem?" asked Jessie. "If you want it so badly, why didn't you get it last night when you saw it?"

"Because my mom and dad wouldn't buy it for me."

"Then why don't you get it with your own money?" asked Robbie. "It's definitely worth spending your own money on."

"I know. I know," I said and sighed. "The problem is this: I don't have enough money in my piggy bank. I need fifty dollars."

"Why don't you do what I do?" Chloe

interrupted. "Ask your grandparents. Whenever my mom and dad won't buy me something, I just ask my nanna for it. She always gets me whatever I want."

"Of course your nanna does," I muttered under my breath.

"You're such a spoiled brat!" Max yelled in her face.

"I am not. I can't help it if my nanna has a lot of money and wants to spend it on me," Chloe said, tossing her fiery red curls and batting her eyelashes.

"Well, not everyone has a rich nanna like that," Jessie said. "I love my *abuela*, but she lives with me and my mom, and she really doesn't have any extra money."

"So what do you do if you want something really bad, and your mom won't buy it for you?" I asked Jessie.

"I do little jobs to earn money. That's how I got my new skateboard."

"My mom and dad said that they would pay me to do chores around the house, but that sounds really boring," I said.

"So think of other things to do that are more exciting," said Jessie.

"Like what?"

"You like animals," Robbie suggested. "You could walk your neighbor's dog. Didn't that nice old lady, Mrs. Golden, who lives two doors down, just break her ankle? You could walk her dog for her every day and take him to play Frisbee in the park."

"That's a good idea."

"You could set up a lemonade stand," Jessie added. "I earned a lot of money selling lemonade, and I had so much fun making the lemonade, setting up the stand, and decorating it with posters."

"Those are great ideas, guys," I said, giving them both a high five. "I think you might be onto something." I was actually starting to get excited about earning money. Walking dogs and selling lemonade sounded a lot better than sweeping the garage. "But do you really think I can earn eighteen dollars in one week? That's a lot of money."

"I think you can do anything you want to do if you just try hard enough," Jessie said, smiling.

"Thanks," I said, smiling back.

Boy, I hope she's right.

CHAPTER 4

If You Have Lemons, Make Lemonade

As soon as I got home from school, I ran down to Mrs. Golden's house. Mrs. Golden has lived on our street forever. She lives by herself and loves when people in the neighborhood stop by to visit. In fact, she often sits on her front porch with her dog, Baxter, a pitcher of lemonade, and a basket of homemade chocolate-chip cookies. She's just waiting for someone to walk by.

Sure enough, when I got to her house today, there she was on the porch, sitting in her favorite rocking chair with her leg in a cast.

"Why, Freddy, what a nice surprise," she said as I came bounding up the porch steps. Baxter started to wag his tail wildly.

"Hi, Mrs. Golden. How's your ankle?" I asked, bending down to pet Baxter's head and rub his belly.

"Oh, it's fine. I'm not as young as I used to be, though," she said with a laugh. "My ankle is going to take some time to heal."

"I'm sure you'll be out of your cast before you know it," I said.

"I hope you're right. Now, how about a cold glass of my special lemonade and a warm chocolate-chip cookie?"

"Well, you know I can never say no to that, Mrs. Golden," I said, grabbing a cookie and shoving it in my mouth. Then I poured myself a glass of lemonade and drank it all in one gulp. "That is the best lemonade in town," I said, smacking my lips and wiping my mouth on my shirtsleeve.

"So, Freddy, what's new?"

"Well, Mrs. Golden, I wanted to ask you a favor . . . actually two favors."

"Really? Well, I'll see what I can do. I don't know how much help I can be with this cast on my leg."

"Having your leg in a cast is actually going to help me out a lot."

"It is?" Mrs. Golden replied, looking confused. "What do you mean?"

"You see, last night I was at the mall, and I went into my favorite store called Treasures of Time."

"Oh, I love that store," Mrs. Golden said. "They have beautiful crystals and gems there."

"Really?" I said in amazement. "I didn't know you had ever been in there before."

"I walk in there every time I go to the mall. I just haven't been there lately because of my leg. It's so hard to move around."

"Well, last night I went there to go look around, and I found this amazing fossilized Megalodon tooth!"

"I'm sorry, Freddy, but I don't know what that is. It sure sounds interesting, though."

"The Megalodon was an ancient shark that was bigger than your house!"

"Wow! Bigger than this house! That's incredible," Mrs. Golden said.

"The fossilized teeth are all that is left of these sharks. You don't see their teeth very often, and I really want one."

"It sounds like a real treasure," Mrs. Golden said, patting me on the back. "I hope you get it before someone else does."

"Well, here's the problem," I continued. "The tooth costs fifty dollars, and I only have thirty-two dollars in my piggy bank. The guy at the store said he'd hold it for me for one week. That means I only have one week to earn eighteen dollars!"

"So how can I help?" Mrs. Golden asked.

"I was hoping that maybe I could walk Baxter for you since you can't take him out right now, and you could pay me to do it." As soon as Baxter heard the word "walk," his tail started wagging like crazy.

"You mean you want to be my official dog walker?" Mrs. Golden said, smiling. "It looks like Baxter certainly likes the idea."

"Yeah," I said, laughing as Baxter started

to lick my face. "I could even take him to the park to play Frisbee."

"Oh, I'm sure he'd love that," Mrs. Golden said. "How does two dollars a walk sound?"

"That sounds great!" I said excitedly. "If I walk him for the next six days, then I'll earn . . . let me see . . . twelve whole dollars."

"You are exactly right," said Mrs. Golden. "So how much more would you need to get that shark tooth?"

"Wait, let me see," I said, counting on my fingers. "I would still need . . . um . . . six dollars."

"And how do you plan on earning the rest of the money?"

"Well, that's where the second favor comes in," I said. "My friends at school told me I should have a lemonade stand, and since you make the best lemonade around, I was hoping that maybe you could help me make the lemonade for my stand. Maybe you'd even tell me your secret recipe."

"For you, Freddy, I would do anything," Mrs. Golden said with a twinkle in her eye. "But you have to swear not to let anyone else in on the secret."

I raised my right hand. "I swear I will never tell anyone the lemonade secret," I said. "My lips are sealed."

"While you are walking Baxter today, I will make a list of ingredients for you to pick up. Then you can come back tomorrow," said Mrs. Golden, "and we'll whip up a batch of the supersecret lemonade. You can even sell it right in front of my house if you like."

"Really? Thanks! You're the best!" I said, giving her a hug.

"I'm just glad I can help."

"You're helping me more than you'll ever know," I said with a big grin. "Last night I never thought I could earn all that money in one week, but now I think I just might be able to do it." I started to put Baxter's leash on him.

"As my daddy always said," Mrs. Golden continued, "'If you've got lemons, then make lemonade.'"

"Huh?" I said, not sure what she meant.

Mrs. Golden started laughing. "It's just an old-fashioned expression that means you can take a bad situation and turn it into something good if you try."

"No wonder you make the best lemonade in town," I called to her as Baxter started pulling me down the steps. "We'll be back in a little while. Start making that list. I can't wait to turn my lemons into lemonade!"

CHAPTER 5

47, 48, 49, 50!

One week later, I was sitting on the floor of my bedroom counting out all the money from my piggy bank. "Forty-seven, forty-eight, forty-nine, fifty!"

"I did it! I did it! I did it!" I yelled, jumping around my room. "Now I have enough to buy the Megalodon tooth!"

"No you don't," Suzie said, sticking her head into my room.

"Yes I do," I snapped back.

"No you don't," Suzie insisted.

"YES I DO!" I screamed at her. I ran to close my bedroom door. "Besides, what are you doing snooping around my room? Stop spying on me!" I said, trying to shove the door closed. "Get out of here!"

"You forgot about tax," Suzie went on, pushing her way into the room.

"What?" I asked.

"Tax."

"Could you speak English, please?"

"Whenever you buy something at a store, you have to pay the amount on the price tag plus the tax," explained Suzie.

"How come no one ever told me that before?!" I yelled. "Great. Just great. Now I don't have enough money to buy the tooth, and my time is up. The guy at the store isn't going to hold it after today."

"Maybe I can help," Suzie said, grinning.

"Oh yeah, right. Just get out. I'm not in the mood for your jokes."

"No, I'm serious," Suzie insisted.

"Well then, spit it out already! How can you help?"

"I can loan you the money for the tax."

"You would do that for me?" I asked, surprised and a little suspicious.

"Of course I would," Suzie answered sweetly. "You're my brother, right? I would do anything in the world for you."

"OK, what's the catch?"

"Why do you think there's a catch?" Suzie said, smiling.

"Because whenever you say you'll do something nice for me, there's a catch."

"Oh, I see I have taught you well, little one," Suzie said.

"So? Tell me. What's the deal this time?"

"The deal is . . . I lend you the money for the tax, and you carry my backpack for a week."

"A week? Are you crazy?" I said.

"I thought you really wanted that dumb shark's tooth."

"I do."

"So . . . do we have a deal or not?" Suzie asked. She held up her right pinkie so we could lock pinkies and pinkie swear.

"A week is a long time. How about if I carry your backpack for a day?"

"A day? Now you're talking crazy," Suzie said. "There's no way I'd lend you the money if you're only going to carry my backpack for one lousy day."

"Two days?" I pleaded.

"I told you what the deal was, and I'm not willing to negotiate," Suzie said, waving her pinkie in my face. "So, for the last time, do we have a deal or not?"

I really didn't want to be Suzie's slave for a whole week, but I just had to have that Megalodon tooth. "Deal," I said, and we locked our pinkies.

"I'll get the money and be right back," Suzie called as she ran out of my room.

Really soon, I was going to have that Megalodon tooth for my very own. I was so excited. I couldn't wait any longer. "Hurry up!" I yelled to Suzie. "I want to get to the mall before it closes."

"I'll be right there," she called back. "Hold your horses, cowboy!"

As soon as Suzie was back with the money, I grabbed it from her, and we ran downstairs to the kitchen.

"Mom, Dad, I have the fifty dollars right

here," I said, jumping around the kitchen. "Can we go to the mall now? Can we? Can we? Can we?"

"Well, Freddy, I sure am proud of you," said my dad. "You worked really hard, and you earned that money all by yourself."

"I am really proud of you, too," said my mom, giving me a big hug. "You were so responsible and you took your jobs very, very seriously. Good work, honey."

"So can we go?" I asked again, tugging on my mom's sleeve. "The store closes in an hour, and the guy's only holding it for me until the end of today."

"Of course we can go," my mom said. "You definitely deserve it."

I raced to the front door. "So what are we waiting for, slowpokes?" I called from the front of the house. "Let's go!"

CHAPTER 6

It's Mine,
All Mine

As soon as we got to the mall, I sprinted to
Treasures of Time, and I almost knocked into
a man coming out of the store.

"Slow down there, honey!" my mom called.
"Watch where you're going."

I was too excited to watch where I was
going. I ran right up to the counter.

"Well, look who's here," said the guy
behind the counter. "Just in the nick of time.

I actually didn't think you were going to make it, kid."

"I made it," I said, panting. I was out of breath from running through the mall. "Did you save it for me?"

"Of course," said the guy. "I promised that I would hold it for one week, and the week wasn't up until closing time today. I have it right here behind the counter."

I was so excited. My heart was beating a million times a minute. I was going to have my very own fossilized Megalodon tooth!

As soon as the guy brought it out, I grabbed it and rubbed my hand over it. It was so cool just to hold it.

"Hold on there, buddy," said the guy. "Your mom and dad have to pay for it first. That's a very delicate fossil. I wouldn't want anything to happen to it."

"Oh yeah, right," I said and laughed. "I have all the money right here." I patted my bulging pocket.

"Oh really? *You* have the money?" The guy sounded surprised.

By then my mom, dad, and Suzie had caught up to me. "Yes, he does," said my dad. "And he earned it all by himself."

"Wow, I'm impressed," said the guy. "That's

a lot of money for a little boy like you. How did you earn that much?"

"I worked hard," I said, smiling. My mom and dad laughed.

"I bet you did."

"I walked my neighbor's dog and sold lots and lots of lemonade."

"Well, good for you," the guy said, patting me on the back. "I wish more kids these days would work for something they really want instead of just having it handed to them. You should be really proud of yourself."

"We're all very proud of him," my mom piped up.

"We're all very proud of him," Suzie said under her breath as she rolled her eyes.

"So, how much do I owe you?" I asked.

"Let's see," said the guy. "May I have it back, please, so I can check the price?"

I carefully handed it back to him, and he rang it up. "That will be fifty-four dollars and thirteen cents."

"Oh no," said my mom.

"What?" I asked.

"Daddy and I forgot to tell you about the tax. I'm so sorry, Freddy."

"That's OK," Suzie chimed in. "I told him all about it and lent him the extra money."

"Really? That was so sweet of you, Suzie," my mom said. "Freddy, you are so lucky to have a big sister like Suzie."

"Yeah, really lucky," I mumbled. If they only knew. But Suzie could pretend she was the Queen of Nice for today. I didn't care. I was in too good a mood to start a fight.

I reached in my pocket and pulled out the crumpled bills. "Here you go, mister. It's all there," I said. I put the money down on the counter.

"It sure is." He opened the cash register. "You are now the official owner of a real fossilized Megalodon tooth. Congratulations, kid. Would you like me to put it in a bag?"

"No thanks. I just want to carry it."

He put the tooth in my hand, and I was so excited. It felt just like Christmas morning. Now it was mine. Really mine.

"Are you sure you don't want a bag?" my mom asked.

"Yeah, I'm sure," I said, clutching the tooth and smiling from ear to ear.

"Well, just be careful you don't drop it," my dad said.

"Don't worry, Dad. I'm going to take really good care of it, I promise."

We left the mall and started to drive home. I sat in the car with a huge grin on my face, rubbing the tooth between my fingers. "I can't wait to take this to school tomorrow and show Robbie," I said.

"What do you mean, take it to school?" my mom asked.

"Yeah, Freddy. What happened to 'Don't worry, Dad. I'm going to take really good care of it'?"

"I meant I wasn't going to lose it."

"Well, I don't think taking it to school is a very good idea," said my mom. "You worked way too hard for this tooth to have anything happen to it."

"Nothing's going to happen to it," I said. "Besides, I promised Robbie that I would bring it tomorrow."

"Why don't you just invite Robbie to come over after school tomorrow and show it to him then?" my mom said.

"I think that sounds like a better idea," my dad agreed.

"No! You don't understand. I want all the kids to see it. I usually don't have something this cool to show off. And since I paid for it with my own money, I can do whatever I want with it."

"Suit yourself," said my mom.

"Yeah, and don't come crying to me when something happens to it," said Suzie.

"Nothing's going to happen to it!" I yelled. "Nothing!"

CHAPTER 7

Look What I've Got!

In the morning, my mom drove us to school, so I couldn't show off my Megalodon tooth on the bus. I had to wait until I got to my classroom, but first I had to carry Suzie's backpack to her room. As soon as we got there, I dropped her backpack on the ground.

"There you go, Brat," I said as I turned to go. "I'm leaving."

"Oh no you're not. You have to hang it up on my hook."

"Sorry, but that wasn't part of the deal," I yelled as I ran off. "You just said I had to carry it!"

"Don't be late to pick it up after school," she called after me. "You have to carry it to the bus, you know."

I ran as fast as I could to my classroom and got there a few minutes before the morning bell rang.

Robbie came running over. "So, Freddy, did you get it?"

"Yep," I said, grinning. "Got it right here." I patted my pocket.

"Well, come on. What are you waiting for? Let me see it!" Robbie said excitedly.

I slowly took the tooth out of my pocket and held it up for Robbie to see. Robbie gasped. "That is sooo cool. Wow! You are so lucky, Freddy."

Just then, some of the other kids in my class came over to see what Robbie was going crazy about.

"Is that it, Freddy?" Jessie asked. "Is that the Megalodon tooth you wanted so badly?"

"It sure is, and I had to work really, really hard to get it."

"I knew you could do it," Jessie said, giving me a high five.

"The lemonade stand was a great idea. I actually had a lot of fun doing it. Maybe we could sell lemonade together sometime."

"That sounds like fun," said Jessie.

Just then Max shoved his way into the group of kids gathered around me. "Hey, what's going on here? What are you all doing? Is Freddy showing you the little teddy bears on his Pull-Ups?"

I could feel my face turn bright red.

"No," Jessie said, turning to look Max right in the eye. "For your information, he's showing us the Megalodon tooth he bought with his own money. Oh, and by the way," she added, "how would you know that Pull-

Ups have teddy bears on them unless you wear them yourself?"

All the kids started giggling. Max's cheeks got as red as a tomato, and he sputtered, "I, I, I do not wear Pull-Ups!"

Boy, Jessie was so brave. She was never afraid to stand up to Max, and she always knew the right thing to say to put him in his place. I wish I could think of things like that to say. I usually think of a good answer hours later when it is too late, and Max has already made a fool of me.

"Did you ask your grandpa and grandma to buy it for you like I told you?" Chloe asked as she came skipping up to join the group.

"No, I worked hard and earned the money all by myself," I said proudly.

"You did?" Chloe said, wrinkling up her nose. "I've never worked for anything I

wanted. Somebody always just gives it to me.
I'm lucky, I guess."

"Well, you should try working for it sometime," I suggested.

"But why would I do that?" Chloe asked.
"That seems so silly."

"It's not silly," I said. "It's actually fun, and
this tooth is even more special to me because
I had to work so hard to get it."

"But if I worked hard, I might just break one of my beautifully painted fingernails." Chloe waved her princess-pink nails in my face. "Aren't they too perfect?"

"Ugh, you are such a spoiled little baby," Jessie said.

"I am not!" Chloe cried, stamping her foot. "I am not a baby."

"Hey, watch it, you little priss," Max said.

"You just stepped on my foot. Let's see how you like it." Then he turned around and stomped on her foot.

"OOOWWW!" she wailed, hopping around on one foot. "OOOWWWW! OOOWWWW! OOOWWW! You are such a meanie, Max Sellars, and you ruined my new patent leather shoes. I'm going to tell Mrs. Wushy," she said and went hopping off into the classroom.

"Chloe is always such a drama queen," Jessie said, laughing.

Max moved around the circle and squished his way in next to me. "Hey, can I hold it, Freddy?" he asked.

Was he crazy? Why would I let Max Sellars, the biggest bully in the whole first grade, hold something this special? Even if I did like him, which I don't, I'm not sure I'd let him hold it. I hadn't even let Robbie hold it, and he is

my best friend. "Umm, I don't think so. It's very breakable. I don't think I'm going to let anyone hold it."

"Oh, come on, Freddy," Max said, reaching for the tooth. "Just for a second."

"Maybe you didn't hear him," Jessie answered, swatting his hand away. "Freddy said 'no.'"

Just then the morning bell rang. Whew, saved by the bell!

"I'll bring it back out again at recess," I told all the kids gathered around me.

We all walked into class, and I went straight to my cubby to put the tooth away for safe-keeping. I didn't want to leave it in my pocket because I was afraid it was going to fall out. I knew it would be safe in my cubby until recess time. I hid it under some papers and went to sit on the rug.

CHAPTER 8

Gone!

The morning work time seemed as if would never end. I couldn't concentrate on math. I just kept thinking about my Megalodon tooth. All the kids in the class thought it was really cool.

Finally, after what seemed like forever, Mrs. Wushy said, "Time for recess, everybody."

I practically threw my paper on her desk and ran to my cubby to get the tooth. I shoved my hand under the papers, but I didn't feel anything. "I must have stuck my hand in the wrong cubby," I thought to myself, so I took a step back to look at the names on the cubbies. Nope, I was in the right cubby. I shoved my hand back in and felt around again. Still nothing. My heart started beating a little faster.

Just then Robbie came over. "Hey, Freddy, you coming out to recess?" he asked. "Don't forget to bring the tooth."

"I'm coming," I said. "I'm just trying to find the tooth."

"What do you mean, trying to find it?"

"Well, I put it under the papers in my cubby this morning when we came in, but now it's not there," I said.

"It's got to be there," Robbie said. "I'm sure it just got stuck in between two of the papers.

Let me check." Robbie lifted up each paper in my cubby, one at a time.

"So?" I asked, looking over his shoulder. "Did you find it? Did you find it?" I was starting to get a little panicked.

"Um . . . It's not here," Robbie answered.

"What do you mean it's not there?" I asked Robbie. I grabbed him by both shoulders and shook him.

"I mean I don't see it."

"Move out of the way," I said, shoving Robbie aside. "It's got to be there!" I was now completely panicked. I threw each paper from my cubby onto the floor until my cubby was completely empty. Still there was no sign of the tooth.

"OH NO! OH NO!" I yelled.

Mrs. Wushy came running over and put

her arm around me. "Freddy, what's the problem? Are you all right?"

"NO! I'M NOT ALL RIGHT!" I screamed. "SOMEBODY STOLE MY MEGALODON TOOTH!"

By now all the kids had heard me screaming, and they came running into the classroom.

"What's going on?" Jessie asked.

"SOMEBODY STOLE MY MEGALODON TOOTH!" I wailed.

"No way!" said Jessie.

"It's true," said Robbie. "We looked all over Freddy's cubby, but it's not there. Somebody in this class took it."

"Well, this makes me very upset," said Mrs. Wushy. "I can't believe that someone in our class would take something that didn't belong to them."

"Max took it!" Chloe blurted out.

"I did not!" Max yelled back.

"I know he took it, Mrs. Wushy," Chloe said, pointing her finger at Max.

"How do you know?" asked Mrs. Wushy. "Did you see him take it?"

"He took it," Chloe repeated.

"You didn't answer my question, Chloe," Mrs. Wushy continued. "Did you actually see him take it?"

"Well . . . ummm . . ."

"No, she didn't see me take it because I didn't take it," said Max.

"Chloe, you can't just go around accusing someone of something unless you saw it with your own eyes. I will ask you one more time, and I want the truth. Did you see Max take it with your own eyes?"

"Ummmm . . . No, not with my own eyes, but . . ."

"Maybe Chloe took it, Mrs. Wushy, and she just doesn't want to get caught," said Max.

"Me? Me? Why would I take it?" Chloe sputtered. "I don't need to steal things. I always get whatever I want, remember?"

"How could we forget," Jessie muttered under her breath.

"MY TOOTH! MY TOOTH!" I sobbed.

"IT'S GONE FOREVER, AND I CAN'T GET ANOTHER ONE! ALL THAT HARD WORK DOWN THE DRAIN!"

Mrs. Wushy gave me a hug. "It's OK, Freddy. Don't cry. We'll find it."

"How? How are you going to find it?" I cried. "You'll never find it!"

"We could call the police and have them dust for fingerprints," Robbie suggested.

"This is not something the police would come out for," said Mrs. Wushy. "I'm afraid we'll have to solve this one on our own."

Mrs. Wushy called everyone back to the rug. "Boys and girls, I am very sad to say that Freddy had something very special stolen from his cubby this morning. This is why I tell you not to bring your special toys and treasures to school. You never know what might happen."

"My mom warned me," I thought to myself. "Oh, why didn't I listen to my mom? If I had just left it at home, then none of this would have ever happened."

"So," Mrs. Wushy continued, "no one is going anywhere until we solve this little mystery. If I have to check everyone's cubbies and backpacks, then I will do that, but I really don't want to. I want the person who took the tooth to stand up and tell the truth. I know that's hard to do, but you will be in less trouble if you admit it than if I find it from my search."

There was silence in the room. You could have heard a pin drop. Everyone was looking around at one another, waiting to see if anyone would admit to it.

Finally, a boy named Charles started sobbing. "I took it, Freddy. I took it! It is so cool. I just wanted it really really badly. I'm sorry. I'm sorry." He took it out of his pocket and handed it to me.

I grabbed it and held it tightly in my hand. "It's OK, Charles," I said. "I'm just glad you gave it back to me."

"I am very disappointed that you took something that didn't belong to you," said

Mrs. Wushy, "but I am proud of you for admitting it. I know that was hard to do. I am still going to have to talk to your parents about this, though. Stealing is a very serious matter. But I know you will never steal again. Right, Charles?"

"No, I won't," Charles said, sniffling. "I promise. Never ever."

"Well," said Mrs. Wushy, "I'm glad that mystery is solved. I hope you all understand how wrong stealing is and how important it is to tell the truth. And, Freddy, from now on, if you have something that valuable, I suggest you leave it at home."

"Don't worry, Mrs. Wushy," I said. "I'm never going to bring something this special to school again."

"Would you like me to keep it in my desk until the end of school?" Mrs. Wushy asked.

"No, that's OK," I said, slipping it into my pocket. "I think I'll just keep it right here. I don't want anything else to happen to it."

"Are you sure, Freddy?"

"Oh, I'm sure," I said, smiling.

In the last week, I had turned enough lemons into lemonade to last a lifetime!

DEAR READER,

I have been a teacher for many years, and I have two kids of my own. I know that there is always something that kids want REALLY, REALLY badly! They just have to have it.

When I was little, Cabbage Patch Dolls were very popular, and I couldn't live without one. I begged my mom and dad to buy one for me, but they said I had to save up for one and buy it with my own money.

I didn't have enough money in my piggy bank, so I had to earn the rest of the money. I had a lemonade stand, and I also put on a magic show with my brother, and I charged the kids in the neighborhood to come see it.

I finally earned enough money to buy the doll. I think she was even more special to me because I had worked so hard to get her.

I bet you have worked hard to buy something special. How did you earn the money, and what did you buy? I'd love to hear about it. Just write to me at:

Ready, Freddy! Fun Stuff
c/o Scholastic Inc.
P. O. Box 711
New York, NY 10013-0711

I hope you have as much fun reading *Shark Tooth Tale* as I had writing it.

HAPPY READING!

Abby Klein

Freddy's Fun Pages

FREDDY'S SHARK JOURNAL

MEGALODON

Megalodon was the biggest predatory shark that ever lived. Its body could be more than 50 feet long.

Megalodon had razor-sharp teeth that could be the size of a human hand. The biggest tooth ever found was almost seven inches long.

Its jaws were so large it could swallow a dolphin.

Megalodon lived in the Earth's oceans until one and a half million years ago. Scientists think that Megalodon looked similar to the Great White Shark— only much larger!

Megalodon teeth have been found in the United States, Australia, New Zealand, and Europe.

ROBBIE'S SHARK QUIZ

1. WHALE SHARKS
   a) are the only sharks that have bones.
   b) have more than 3,000 teeth but only eat microscopic plankton.
   c) run out of teeth when they are 42 years old.

2. GREAT WHITE SHARKS
   a) live in cold climates where their color blends in with snow and ice.
   b) are the smallest species of shark.
   c) have teeth that are notched like saws.

3. BLUE SHARKS
   a) can swim one mile in 103 seconds.
   b) lie on the ocean floor looking for lobsters.
   c) have been known to eat their own young.

4. HAMMERHEAD SHARKS
   a) are often seen in large schools of hundreds.
   b) have teeth covering their dorsal fins and heads.
   c) are closely related to Nailhead Sharks.

5. STETHACANTHUS SHARKS
   a) lived 360 million years ago.
   b) have a sucking disk on the top of their head.
   c) live in warm waters off Australia.

6. MAKO SHARKS
   a) have been known to eat swordfish whole.
   b) live in freshwater rather than salt water.
   c) are allergic to bees.

7. You are most likely to see a shark if
   you swim in waters near:
   a) Alaska
   b) Japan
   c) Australia

8. The following statements are true or false:
   a) The shark is the only fish that can blink its eyes.
   b) Most sharks have very good color vision.
   c) Some sharks lay eggs, and others give birth to
      live young.

9. Pick the correct word:
   a) a single shark can replace
   (10,000, 30,000, 100,000, 250,000) teeth.
   b) sharks have teeth in many
   (places, rows, dark spots).
   c) sharks have been around for
   (2,000, 10 million, 450 million, a billion) years.

ANSWERS

1: b; 2: c; 3: a; 4: a; 5: a; 6: a; 7: c; 8a: T; 8b: T; 8c: T;
9a: 30,000; 9b: rows; 9c: 450 million

93

TURNING LEMONS INTO LEMONADE!

Shhh . . . Can you keep a secret? Here's Mrs. Golden's secret recipe for the best lemonade ever! Always remember to get an adult to help you when using knives and heating water!

Mix in a pitcher:

½ cup sugar

½ cup water (heated)

Add:

juice of 2–3 lemons

½ lemon, thinly sliced

1 quart (4 cups) of cold water

12 ice cubes

Stir with a wooden spoon.
Pour into glasses and enjoy!

FREDDY'S SECRET CODE

Use the code below to answer these questions about Megalodons.
—Freddy

a	e	f	h	g	l	n	o
☺	*	%	▲	?	♥	◆	#

p	r	s	t	u	w	y
=	@	→	$	●	+	☒

What does the name Megalodon mean?

? @ * ☺ $　$ # # $ ▲

Some Megalodons weighed as much as:

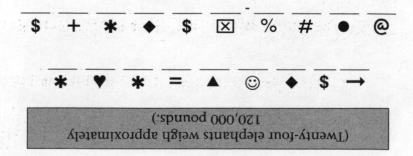

$ + * ◆ $ ☒ - % # ● @

* ♥ * = ▲ ☺ ◆ $ →

(Twenty-four elephants weigh approximately
120,000 pounds.)

95

Have you read all about Freddy?

Freddy will do anything to lose a tooth fast!

Freddy's found the best show-and-tell ever!

Freddy's research turns up some unexpected results!

Can Freddy overcome Max the bully?

Help! Does anyone have a magic spell for talent?

Can Freddy find a way to make the vampire go away?

Yikes! Can Freddy learn to ride a bike in less than two weeks?

It's Halloween, but Freddy is afraid of ghosts and goblins!

Don't miss Freddy's next adventure!